PART 1
"Section 1"

Help! He's crazy! The children stood there, watching as their godmother Cathy, went through pure torture. Their mother, Angie was at work and their father, Bryan was out on a business trip. Cathy was in charge of keeping an eye on the kids until their mother came home from work. Angie was a real estate agent by day and stripper by night. Her husband Bryan was a pharmaceutical sales representative, he never made time for Angie and the kids. The two of them bore three children; Julian age seven, Clarissa age five and Miracle who had just turned six months old. They adopted their God son Adrian about a year ago, his mother died in a car crash the day after his fifteenth birthday and he never really knew his father.

Adrian was a big help with the kids, until he fractured his knee in basketball. He was an all around athlete and honor student, stood at 6'1 and weighed a little over 200 pounds. Angie and Bryan didn't want to add anymore stress on his shoulders, so they hired Cathy to keep an eye on the kids. Cathy was a middle aged white woman, nicely dressed, very clean and had some classiness about herself. She lived alone and was pregnant once, but lost the baby at three months due to ongoing work ethics. Years later, she retired and has been alone ever since. So they figured, her watching the kids earning a few extra dollars, would be exactly what she needed.

Angie became a stripper about five years ago after graduating college. When she met Bryan her life changed, they got married and then she was pregnant a year later with Julian. Things were so smoothe in the beginning, they always made time for one another, Julian was the best thing that ever happened to them. Bills weren't a hassle, because she had saved up so much money from dancing, she could buy her and her husband a house and still had money to spare. Angie was about 5'5, 150 pounds, long black hair and had curves in all the right places.

Bryan and her met on the downtown strip in Atlanta. She was having a drink at a poetry lounge, called "The Spot". He walked in with his business attire and all she saw was a handsome set of muscles. Bryan stood at 6'3 about 230 pounds, dreadlocks neatly twisted, that touched the middle of his back and beautiful white teeth. They made eye contact and it was history from there. Later, they began having problems after Clarissa was born. She went through Bryan's phone and saw that he had been meeting up and chatting with another woman from Nashville, TN, during one of his many "business trips".

She never addressed the situation, but instead she became a stripper by night to get the attention from other men that she wasn't getting from her husband. After Miracle was born, they really needed the money anyway. Angie's nights at the strip club were the best, her private room dances, made her about $3000/night, maybe even a little more, if she liked the customer and needed an orgasm. It had been so long, since her and Bryan were intimate, she missed the feeling. Her stage performances were the best ! In one night, she brought in close to $10,000 and although she popped out three children, she still had the body of the goddess. One night on the way to her car, two of the other strippers tried to jump her.

Little did they know, they would be left bloody and broken. She kept a blade in her bra, stabbing one of them in the ribs and breaking the other's nose. Angie practiced martial arts for three and a half years while she was in college and kickboxed for one year, although she was a bit older, the techniques never left her. When she finally made it home, the kids were sound asleep in their beds and Cathy would be awake feeding Miracle her bottle. Angie would grab Miracle and let Cathy get some rest, she enjoyed that time with her babygirl. Walking into an empty room and empty bed became normal for her, so she would play with her baby until she fell asleep. Then she would run herself a hot bubble bath, put on some slow jams and relax. She would get out of the tub, put on her lace panties and bra, with her silk robe and count all the money she made for the night.

"Section 2"

The next morning, Angie is awakened by a text from Bryan at 9 am. The message said, *" hey beautiful, I just wanted to tell you, I love you and I will be home tonight around 7pm, my plane lands at 6pm, but I have to go by the office to drop off some papers. Hope you enjoy the gift out front."*

Angie looks over at her daughter, seeing that she is still sound asleep, she goes to the kitchen and fixes herself a hot cup of coffee. She turned on the news and puffed her vape pen. After she finished drinking her coffee, she looked out the front window and saw that Bryan had a brand new Mercedes truck delivered to their house for her as a gift. She smirked a little bit and went back to watching her news and poured herself another cup of coffee. In the back of her mind, she knew she had enough money of her own, to buy herself a Mercedes truck. But she was content with her two door drop top convertible and the minivan she drove, when she wanted to take the kids on an outing.

This new truck must have been Bryan's way of apologizing for being gone for two weeks and not calling or answering any of my calls, Angie thought to herself. In his mind he thought that buying her nice things would keep her happy, when he would do wrong. It used to work when things were fresh between them, but along the way she learned that money can't buy happiness. Little did he know, she had plans the same night with her sugar daddy and he would see how it feels to lie in a king size bed alone. Bryan was good with the kids and when he was home, they hated to see him leave. He made over $75,000/year and brought them whatever their hearts desired.

He kept two phones, the other, he didn't think Angie knew about. Clarissa was going through his briefcase and started pretending as if she was talking to someone on his brand new blackberry.She seen it, when she hopped out of the shower and when she asked him about it, he lied and said it was a business phone for work, to keep up with his clients. She simply replied *"okay honey"* and kept going on about her day. Bryan had no idea she would go to Walmart the following day and bought a brand new smartphone, alot bigger than Bryan's phone. Of course, she still had her original phone, but she needed another line for 'business purposes'.

That evening, Bryan's plane landed at approximately 6:15pm, he turned his phone back on and saw that Angie never replied. He received three text messages from his homeboy Evon. The first message read, *"Aye, Bryan when you land, hit me up. I'm thinking about hitting up 'Juicy' tonight. We need to get out and have some drinks while you are in town, you know it has been awhile."*

Bryan looked at the message and laughed to himself. He couldn't fix himself to tell Evon he had a romantic evening planned for him and his wife. He tried calling Angie, but it went straight to her voicemail *"this is Angie, leave a message after the beep."* He got to the office, dropped off his paperwork and tried to reach her again, but it was still going to her voicemail. He drove home and when he pulled up in the drop top Bentley, he saw the minivan and the brand new Mercedes, but didn't see Angie's convertible. He walks in the house and Cathy is cooking dinner for the children. When they saw their father walk in, they frantically ran to him screaming "daddy!" He embraced them and gave them each some money to put in their piggy banks. He reached down and grabbed Miracle as she was drooling all over her toy in her bouncer. He walked into the kitchen greeting Cathy as she multitasked fixing plates and finalizing her dish to feed the children and get them bathed and into bed, before 9pm.

He asks Cathy *"have you heard from Angie? I have been trying to call her phone since I landed, it sends me straight to voicemail, that's normally not like her."* She looked at him and said *"no, she told me she was going to be coming in late tonight to pull some over time at work. Now please get out of my kitchen with that baby and this grease is everywhere, you see I'm getting dinner ready for these kids."* Bryan laughed and went to the other room to play with Miracle and give her a bath to put on her night clothes for bed.

He checked the other two messages from Evon and it read *"meet me at 'Juicy's' by 9:30, drinks are on me tonight playboy lol."* The last message read *"I don't want to hear no shit man, bring your ass!"*

After he gave Miracle her bath, he fed her a warm bottle and rocked her to sleep. He looked at his blackberry and saw he had a call from Denise (the Nashville girlfriend). He turned the phone off and tried calling Angie again, by this time it was 8;30pm and still no answer from his wife. He went back in the front and saw that the kids had eaten. Clarissa and Julian were in bed and Adrian was in the den playing Madden on his brand new game system. Cathy, was tidying the kitchen and cleaning off the table. She asked Bryan *"is Miracle asleep?"* He replied, *"yes ma'am."* And she proceeded with her evening and headed to the shower.

As Cathy was walking away, she turned to look at Bryan, with worry in her eyes and asked *"are you okay young man?"*

He simply responded *"no I haven't heard from Angie since I landed, did she say how late she was coming in tonight?"*

Cathy replied, *"no she did not."*

Of course Cathy knew about Angie's side hustle, but wasn't going to let Bryan know a thing. She also had Angie's other cell phone number, but wasn't going to give that out either. She paid her extra to keep her mouth shut and watch the kids and she did just that.

"Section 3"

When Bryan realized he wasn't getting a response from his wife, he decided to take Evon up on his offer. He took a quick shower, threw on a white tee shirt, some jeans and tennis shoes and headed out the door. He hits the expressway and pulls up to the hot new spot 'Juicy' and see's Evon outside the building waving to him to come inside. The building was all black with purple letters on the front named 'Juicy'. When they walked in, the club was two stories, with a balcony for VIPs. To the right there were strippers in cages and to the left is an open bar. In the middle of the floor, there was a light reflecting off th black walls, making the room look exotic. The center stage was full of older and middle aged men throwing money to the stripper in the middle of the floor.

Evon had a table set up already with hot wings, fruit, chips and dip, with plenty of liquor bottles. A stripper named "cupcake" came to the table with long black hair down to her ass cheeks, a pink bra and a g-string to match. She even had on platform all black heels. She was such a pretty mixed breed, she had full lips and grey eyes, definitely Bryan's type. She leaned toward Bryan and whispered in his ear *"I want you."* She felt the arousal in his pants, bent over and clapped her booty, grinded on him a little and proceeded to take off her bra. Cupcake was very tempting to Bryan, but all he could think about was Angie, so he gave her $1,300 and sent her on her way.

He glared at the centerstage, to see what the hype was about, but couldn't really get a good look, so he stood up. He wondered why all these men were surrounding this one woman. Evon noticed Bryan glaring at the stage and he says *"aw yea that's sweetie...on stage, word is she breakin niggas pockets, she does wonders on the scene and behind the scenes, if you know what I mean."*

Bryan replied, *"is that right?"* As he's walking toward the stage, wondering what she's like behind the scenes. Sweetie had on anexotic mask that covered her eyes, when Bryan got a little closer, she had on just a lace thong and the way she bent over, he could see the piercing on her cliterous. She wore a pair of black lace gloves and climbed the pole in such an exotic way. She worked her way back down smoothly, landing into a full split.

The guys went crazy and threw more money, she made eye contact with Bryan and gave him a small smirk. She bent her legs into a full chinese slit and crawled her way to the other side of the stage. When she turned around, he noticed the butterfly tattoo in the middle of her back, with two chinese symbols on her lower back. Bryan thought to himself…._"this cannot be my wife"_ and laughed to himself. She then climbed off the stage and onto a man's lap and he noticed the heart birthmark on her left thigh. Things weren't quite funny anymore, he screamed her name and the entire club stopped, but she kept dancing. Bryan ran across the stage and snatched his wife off of the man's lap and out the door. She fought him off of her and screamed _"what the fuck are you doing ?!"_

He pent her against the side of the building and looked at her with anger in his eyes and asked her _"What the fuck are you doing here?! You are my wife and this is how you portray yourself?"_

Angie looked into his eyes and said, _"oh so now you realize, you have a wife or that I am your wife ? After all your many"business" trips you take to see that bitch in Nashville."_

Bryan put his head down… Angie picks his chin up and looks into his eyes. _"Yea that's what I thought, get the fuck outta my way so that I can finish making my money!"_

Bryan snatches her back. _"You got me fucked up, if you think I'm just gonna let you just walk back in there!"_ Angie looks back and says _"you don't have a choice Bryan, you disappear for weeks at a time and I don't even get a simple 'I love you', maybe you will enjoy sleeping in a big king size bed alone."_

She jerks away from him and Bryan grabs her by the waist and throws her against the wall, he glares into her soul as her eyes filled with rage. Evon runs outside yelling at Bryan, *"aye what you doin man, you gone get us banned from here!"*

He looked to his left, to see Bryan holding Angie aka 'Sweetie" and his eyes grew wide, as in disbelief that sweetie was the woman that Bryan married. She looked back at her husband and said, *"we will talk about this later, at least let me get the rest of the money that I earned tonight."*

He grabs her by the wrist and says *"you didn't earn that money."*

She snatches away, filled with anger and hurt, he guards the door as he watches her go in and get her bag and scrapes the money in handfuls putting it in a duffel bag. As she gathers all her earnings, she listens to the men 'boo' her as she walks off the stage. She goes to the dressing room and throws on a black jogging suit and Nike tennis shoes, snatches the wig off of her head and throws her hair into a ponytail and heads out the door.

"Section 4"

Bryan walks Angie to the car and as he opens the door for her, a couple guys bomb rushed him, knocking him into the car trying to get to 'Sweetie'. She thought that changing her disguise would have thrown people off, but those two guys saw everything. Bryan was licensed to carry a gun, he pulled the pistol and shot one guy in the leg and the other guy in the arm. Bryan yells at Angie, *"hurry up and drive off!"*

As he approached his vehicle, the two men lay on the ground in pain. Evon ran back inside the club, when the men came out of the door, he knew what time it was. The man with the wounded arm tried chasing after Bryan's car and pulled his gun to begin shooting, but by the time he could cock his gun, Bryan had already made it down the block. Bryan caught up with Angie and trailed her all the way back home, both of them hitting 80 mph on the expressway.

When they finally reached their house, Angie rushed past him to unlock the door, he came in behind her yelling. *"This is your damn fault, had you not been at that damn club, none of this would have happened!"* Angie replied, *"Now this is my fault? Nobody told you to come to the club tryna be a big bad bodyguard anyway Bryan! If you had been home taking care of your kids, being a husband to your wife, none of this would be going on now."*

Bryan Looked at her, like he wanted to hit her, but he knew what his wife was capable of. He slams his fist into the wall and Cathy walks in. *"What is going on here?"*

They both yelled *"Nothing!"*

Seconds later, Clarissa walks in crying and that infuriates Cathy, because all of the children were sleeping just fine, she picks up Clarissa and says to Angie and Bryan *"you two need to get a hold of yourselves, look at what you're doing to the children!"*

Cathy walks off and grabs Clarissa by the hand to tuck her back into bed. Angie looked at Bryan and simply said *"I'm leaving for a couple nights to get my head together, I don't understand how you don't see anything wrong with your actions as well and I am not dealing with your temper tonight Bryan."*

He gets in her face and firmly says *"Angie you're not going anywhere, you are my wife!"*

He stands in front of the door, she gives him this evil eye and says in rage *"you better move Bryan, before I move you and that door too!"*

He knew what that look meant and knew his wife's temper had no remorse, but that's why he loved her so much. He slowly glided toward her, away from the door and whispered *"ight Angie"* and walked around him, he tried to grab her by the arm, but she jerked away from him and headed to her car.

He yelled *"Angie where are you going?"* She looked at him for a moment as she put the car in reverse to pull out of the driveway, she turned her music up and sped away. Thirty minutes later, she pulls up to the Hilton hotel, she grabs her tote with her belongings and hands valet her keys to park her car. She walks inside and she is greeted by a white male at the desk.

"Hello, welcome to the Hilton, this weekend all of our guests get 10% off of everything in the hotel, including souvenirs and rooms." Angie says *"thanks I'll have the master suite king size bed for two nights please."*

He searches on the computer to check for availability.

"Yes we have one available, what is the name on the room?"

13

She hands him her ID. *"Alright Mrs. Tanley the total is $420.77, will you be paying cash or card?"*

She hands him a gold debit card, he slid her card and grabbed the receipt and handed it back to her. Then he reaches in the drawer and hands her the hotel room key. *"Have a good night ma'am."*

Angie didn't respond, she nodded her head and proceeded to walk toward the elevator. When she finally gets to her room, she sits down at the desk and begins to cry and scream. She was so hurt and confused, she never wanted any of this to happen. To ease her mind, she ordered room service and the hotel's most expensive bottle of wine. She ran herself a hot bubble bath, pinned her hair up, got in the tub and had herself a glass of wine. When she finished her time of meditation, she got out of the tub and looked at her phone. She saw that she had five missed calls, all of them from Bryan. She read all eighteen messages about how much he loves her and doesn't want to lose her. She turned her phone off, dried her body off, put her robe on and poured herself another glass of wine.

She turned on the flat screen TV, but there was nothing interesting on, that caught her attention, so she turned it off. She stuffed her face with fruit, food and wine right before she laid down, she texted Cathy from her other line to let her know that she was okay. *"Hey Cathy, I am at a hotel*

. I needed to get away from Bryan. The other phone is turned off, because he kept calling and texting. I need some time to think, he wasn't supposed to find out at all, especially not like this. It's out there now I guess, but anyway you're

doing a great job with the kids and I want you to know how much I appreciate you for being my friend and for helping us out. Let me know if you need anything, kiss the kids for me."

Cathy called Angie a couple days later to check on her, because she hadn't heard from her since she sent that text the night of the fight. When Angie answered the phone, she seemed more happy than she was a couple days ago, Cathy thought to herself.

Part 2

"Section 5"

"Hey girl, I was just calling to check on you, how are you?"

"I'm doing good, just had some time to relax and get my head together. Is everything alright, are the kids okay?

"Yes Angie, everything is fine, I havet heard from you since the altercation with you and Bryan, I was just checking on you."

"Thanks Cathy, you don't know how much I appreciate you. How are the kids and what are they doing?"

"The kids are fine, Julian is studying for his spelling test, Clarissa is playing with her blocks, Miracle is in her swing napping and Adrian went around to the rec center to workout that knee of his."

"That's good, where is Bryan and how did Adrian get to the rec center?"

"Bryan offered to take him there, so they could spend a little more time together. They have actually been inseparable

since you left. He said after he picked him up from the gym, they were going to grab a bite to eat and take him to pick out some new shoes."

Angie had a shocked look on her face, because she had been stressing to him how important it is for him and Adrian to build a stronger bond. With him not being around, he needs guidance when Bryan's around. Knowing that he actually took the initiative to do this, put an even bigger smile on Angie's face.

"Okay I'm on my way back to the house, do you need anything?"

Cathy replied *"yes, can you pick me up a bottle of that nice red wine that you drink and a pizza for the kids? I promised them pizza for being so well behaved."*

The kids yelled *"yay pizza!"*

"Yes, I can get the red wine, but you don't have to treat them to pizza Cathy you have done enough by far! I am going to get them some things and I will just treat them to pizza this evening at chuck e cheese, just make sure they have their shoes on. I have a few errands to run and afterward I want to take my babies shopping, just don't mention chuck e cheese to them."

Cathy laughed and replied *"okay."*

They hung up the phone, a few minutes later, Angie was pulling up with the bottle of wine that Cathy asked for. She looks out of the window before she gets out of the car and sees Clarissa and Julian run to the window with excitement. She walks into the house, hands Cathy the wine that she asked for, she washes her hands and reaches into her purse and hands her five $100 bills, then writes her a check for $1200 and lets her off for the next five days. Cathy was shocked to see the amount of money that Angie paid her, considering Bryan had just given her $600.

"You take this check and go enjoy yourself Cathy, you deserve it."

Cathy replied, *"thank you"* as she leaned in to give Angie a hug.

"What's up with the wine, you got a hot date or something girl?"

Cathy replies *"yea a little something like that."*

"So what is his name then, I need details honey!"

They both laughed, sometimes Cathy forgets that they are still best friends before anything. She then replied *"his name is Chris, he's about 6'3, 215 pounds of all muscle, he asked me on a date tonight and I took the offer."*

"Okay girl, I see you finally trying to get rid of them cobwebs!" They both laughed.

"So how did you encounter this Chris guy and how long have you all been talking?"

"We have been talking for about three months now, he works all the time, so this is our very first date and I'm excited!"

Angie smiled and replied *"okay girl, what does he do for a living and where did you say you met him again?"*

Cathy grinned, overlooking the question and replied *"he works as a truck driver and he's a male nurse, I met him on this dating site."*

Angie looks at Cathy in shock and says, "a dating site Cathy, why are you looking for men on dating sites? *Are you sure this guy is who he says he is Cathy? I mean really, you could be dating a serial killer with a hidden identity or something!"*

Cathy's smile left her face and she became defensive with Angie.

"Look, you don't know him okay, he's kind, sweet and actually likes me for me!" She begins to walk toward her tan two door Jaguar, then Angie stops her.

"Look I know I don't know him, but I'm just looking out for you, I don't want to see you hurt again Cathy."

"Angie I don't jump into your business when it comes to your life or give my opinion on anything, so I suggest you show me the same respect!"

Cathy gets in her car, slams her door and drives away. Angie walked back into the house, grabbed the keys to the minivan, loaded up the kids and headed to the mall. As Angie and the kids are heading to the mall, she encounters a wreck on the highway, which has the traffic backed up and the kids are getting restless. Her phone rings and it's Bryan, she answers the phone and speaks in a calm tone.

"Hey Bryan, I'm glad you called, we need to talk."

He replies *"yes I was thinking the same thing, that's why I called. Where did you go the other night Angie?"*

"I went to the Hilton for a couple nights to clear my head."

Bryan begins to wonder if anyone else met her there, but hesitates to ask, so he changes the subject instead. *"So Angie where are you now? I hear the kids in the background, so I know you have been home."*

"We're on the way to the mall right now and after, I have a little surprise for the kids. We will probably meet you at home, where's Adrian?"

"He's right here, we did some running around today ourselves and now we're about to grab a bite to eat."

Just as the conversation was starting to get a little deeper, Cathy beeps in and she places Bryan on hold. Before Angie could say a word, Cathy just started talking.

"Look Angie I didn't mean to be a bitch, I know you were just looking out for me. I just don't want to think about anything negative to mess up my night, I mean you are right it has been a long time and I was everything to be perfect, well damn near perfect."

"Section 6"

Angie replies, *"I wasn't trying to be negative, I was just saying, the people off the internet can act like one person and end up being someone completely different in person. I just don't want anything to happen to you Cathy. Bryan is on the other line, I'll call you right back in ten minutes.*

She hangs up and clicks back over, *"sorry Bryan that was Cathy, what were you saying?"*

Bryan smiled and said, *"tonight will only be about me and you, that's what I was saying Mrs. Tanley."*

Angie smiled, he always knew how to make her feel butterflies just like the first day they met and that's why she loved him so much. He hangs up the phone and Angie calls Cathy back.

Cathy answers and continues the conversation *"I know you don't want anything to happen to me Angie, but give him a chance with me just once...can you start by helping me choose what to wear tonight."*

Angie sighs, *"sure why not, where's he taking you?"* *"I don't know, he says it's a surprise, so I really don't know how to dress."*

Cathy's always been a plain Jane type of chick, but she was never lazy with her appearance and kept her hair and nails done frequently. She just had brown streaks added to her blonde hair and a few inches chopped off a few weeks ago.

"Meet me at the mall honey, so we can pick you out something nice. I'll drop the kids off in the play area of the mall and just meet me at New York and Company, right across from PlayLand."

Cathy replies *"okay I will meet you there in about an hour, I have to get a fill-in and Jeff is expecting me at any moment to get a quick trim and flat iron."*

"Girl you sure have a lot to do before tonight, where did he want you to meet him?"

"He told me to meet him onLake Street at the French tower about 9pm."

Angie looks at the time on her watch. *"Oh, it's just 3:57pm, you have plenty of time, so get off this phone and handle your business girl. By the time you get to the mall, I will already have an outfit purchased, all you will have to do is throw it on and be on your way honey!"*

Cathy says, *"thanks girl, you're the best, see you in a bit!"*

They hang up the phone and Cathy runs into her house to grab her make up and some jewelry. She stayed in a two bedroom townhouse, with nice interior decorating, she hired someone that Jeff referred her to, whom he's been friends with for several years. He stepped into her home and added some style to her plain little home. He started in one room and she loved how he patterned the floral arrangements,so she let him do the rest of her home. Each room had its own setting and that was the goal she aimed for the most. Her bedroom was yellow and turquoise with a queen size bed, which she hadn't been able to lay in a couple months. Brown and white living/dining room, beige and gold guest room and a green and white kitchen.

Cathy rushes back to her car and finds a note in the windshield. *" You were always beautiful, more beautiful now than you were before."*

Your Secret Admirer

Her stomach dropped, wondering who could have written that note from the time she went into her home and came out . She began to wonder if someone was watching her and if so, because she hadn't met Chris and he didn't know her address. Cathy was a very discrete woman and never gave her private location, because that was her place of peace and solitude. She didn't let that distract her from what she already had on her mind to do. She pulls up to a place called *"Glisson"*, this was her favorite salon and Jeff was waiting at the door with his hand on his hip. She already knew what that meant, Jess was impatient and he was pissed.

   She walks in and smiles, Jeff immediately says *"Miss Catherine, my time belongs to noone, but ME honey, you are thirty minutes late and I was just about to leave. I had plans on being out of the shop by 5pm and laid up with Steve watching 'The Devil Wears Prada' by 6:30pm. The next time, I'm going to close up shop and you have to catch me another day."*

   Cathy smiles and nods her head *"okay Jeff, I'll throw you something extra for holding you up, you know you're my favorite."*

   It takes Jeff about 45 minutes to do her hair, considering she was just in his chair a few weeks ago, so she didn't need much work. He washed her hair, blow dried it and flat ironed it. She headed out the door to go get her fill-in, but when she pulled up to the nail shop, Suzanne was already gone for the day. She turns back around and heads to the mall, she looks at the clock and sees that it's only 6pm, so she just decides to get her nails done at the mall before she tries on the dress, since she had some time to spare.

Cathy calls Angie, *"hey girl I'm on my way to the mall, to try on the dress and to get a fill in. I was late getting to Suzanne, so by the time I got there, she was gone for the day."*

"Okay cool, the kids are eating soft pretzels and I am walking up to New York and Company as we speak."

They hang up the phone and she leaves Julian and Clarissa across the hall at Playland and takes Miracle with her into the store. She walks inside and instantly sees the perfect outfit, a red dress that came a little above the knee to show some thigh, with lace covering the back, a black blazer and red bottom pumps. She places the items on the counter and the total comes out to be $215.91.Just as soon as she walks out of the store Bryan calls.

"What do you want for dinner tonight baby? I prefer you, but I guess we can get to that later."

Angie laughs and says *"honestly lobster sounds great tonight and for dessert, I would like a scoop of you with a cherry on top."*

"Section 7"

Bryan laughs and in a sensual voice says *"you know it has been awhile Angie and I been reminiscing about the way that thang tastes, just like when we first met remember that night at the cabin?"*

"Yes, I remember, how could I forget? The way you touch me, makes my body quiver. Your kisses make me melt and I crave you, when you're not around. Oh, but that night at the cabin, you made me cum three times back to back with a

strawberry and made love to me over and over again. You kissed every inch of my body and held me until I fell asleep."

"And I wanna make you feel those things again Angie. I feel like I have a lot of making up to do and I know that one night won't fix everything, but I don't want to lose you or my family and I will do whatever it takes. I can start by using that cherry tonight, the way I used the strawberry, with your legs on my shoulders."

"Stop it Bryan, you know I'm in public with the kids."

"Yea I know, so how long will it be, before you get to the house?"

"It will be around 9:30, I'm taking the kids to chuck e' cheese, I promised them pizza tonight. It may be about 10pm just to be on the safe side."

"Alright, I will see you tonight baby, I love you with all my heart Mrs. Tanley."

She smiled real big and tears grew in her eyes as she replied *"I love you too Brian."*

Just as they hung up the phone, Cathy called.

"Her girl, are you still here, I just finished getting my nails done."

"Yea I'm still here I just paid for it and it is so sexy girl, you're going to love it!"

"I'm excited honey, here I am !"

Cathy walks up to Angie and she hands her the bag, she rushes to the fitting room to change. It was 7:45, Angie rushed across the hall to the play area, to grab Clarissa and Julian,they didn't want to leave, but they had to. Fifteen minutes later,

Cathy's walking out of the fitting room with her lace red dress and blazer, stilettos and some accessories. She looked like a brand new woman, with the biggest smile, she looked at Angie and said *"this is a beautiful dress girl, I love it Angie!"*

She smiled and said *"you're welcome Cathy, now hurry up it's 8:15pm, you're going to be late, don't keep the man waiting on the first date."*

They laughed as Cathy hugged them goodbye. She always wore a particular fragrance, it was something really soft and it stuck to her wherever she went.

"I'll call and let you know how everything goes, I promise!"

Angie goes into the children's store, she purchased each of the children three outfits a piece. When she looked up, it was already ten minutes to 9pm, the kids had an hour to play at chuck e' cheese before they closed, luckily it was only a block away from the mall. She walks into Chuck e' cheese and orders a pepperoni and cheese pizza, drinks and $20 worth of tokens for Julian and Clarissa to play, which wouldn't take them long to run through them. Once the tokens were gone, they were going home. She couldn't wait for her night with Bryan, that's all she could think about. It had been so long since he touched her and spent quality time with her, she craved him more than he would ever know.

Bryan and Adrian had finished their evening, so he took him to the house, to drop off his bags. They had already discussed earlier that day that he would be staying at Nina's house for a couple days, since he hadn't been out of the house, since his injury. Nina and Adrian had been childhood sweethearts, both their families knew one another very well and they enjoyed having Adrian over. When they pull up to Nina's house, before he gets out, Bryan stops him.

"Did you enjoy yourself today dude?"

"Yea it felt pretty good to get out of the house and get some fresh air, thanks for the shoes by the way."

"You welcome man, I'm proud of you boy, you know I got you, call me tomorrow at 2pm and I'm going to swing by and pick you up, I got another surprise for you."

"Alright pops, I'll call you."

Bryan smiled, because Adrian never called him anything close to dad and he remained very distant since his mother's accident. He was very close to Angie and he told her everything, so having one on one time with him really meant alot to Bryan. He waited for him to get out of the car and into the house, before he pulled off, when he saw that Adrian got into the house, he blew the horn and pulled away.

He headed to Wal-mart, to pick up some candles and rose petals, he looked down at his watch and it was 9:20pm. He still had enough time to pick up the wine and set up their bedroom for the evening. He stopped by their favorite seafood restaurant 'See Seafood' to pick up the lobster tails and sides that he pre-ordered. He pulls back up to the house at exactly 9:45. He grabs the items, gets out of the car and walks into the house, sits the bags down and proceeds to take his shoes off. He heads to the bathroom and runs Angie a nice hot bubble bath with rose petals and her favorite wine on the side of the tub, sitting on ice. He goes to Angie's lace drawer, where she kept all her lingerie and sexy apparel. He loved her scent and the way her body looked in lace, anything looked sexy on her in Bryan's eyes really. He chooses her a sexy lace see thru green onesie, that formed a string in the back for her booty.

"Section 8"

He lays the lingerie across the bed and proceeds to sprinkle rose petals all over the room, from the door to the bed and bathroom. He heads to the kitchen to get two wine glasses and to warm up the food, while the chocolate is melting on the stove. He calls Angie.

"Hey baby, how much longer will you be?"

"It'll be about 20 minutes, before I get home. I'm putting the kids in the car as we speak."

"Okay baby take your time, I'll see you shortly."

They hung up the phone, he knew it wouldn't be a hassle to get the kids asleep once they got home. They loved Chuck e' cheese and they would likely be passed out by the time they got in the car. Angie gets in the car and places the to-go boxes on the floor board and heads to the house, she couldn't wait to see what he had up his sleeve tonight. She looked at the time and saw that it was 10:15, but Bryan knew whenever she took the kids on an outing, she was never on time coming back home. That's one of many reasons she married him, because he knew her better than she knew herself sometimes. She pulled up to the house at 10:35, Bryan came outside to help her with the bags and got the kids inside and in the bed, all of them were full, happy and asleep, just as he suspected. Angie lies Miracle in her crib next to Clarissa's bed and puts the pacifier in her mouth. Brian had already laid Clarissa down in her bed and Julian didn't make it to his room, just passed out on the couch fully clothed.

She heads to the bedroom to shower and relax, but as she approaches the door, she sees the trail of rose petals leading to the room. She turns around in shock and looks at her husband, wanting to cry. He looks at her, kisses her lips and says *"keep walking beautiful."* She opens the door and her mouth drops, to the left there's a bottle of wine on ice with a bowl of cherries and a bottle of whipped cream on the bed. She sees the lingerie he picks out for her, with the covers pulled back and rose petals are just everywhere. She looks at the table counter clockwise from the bed and sees two plates with lobster tail, asparagus and loaded baked potatoes. She smiles and Bryan grabs her from behind and kisses her neck and slides a brand new diamond necklace around her neck. He spins her around, looks into her eyes and says *"I love you Mrs. Tanley, you will always and forever be the love of my life, through the good, bad, sickness and health."*

Tonight was all about rekindling their love again and showing one another that their marriage is worth saving and not giving up. He leads her to the bathroom and she sees the bathtub filled with bubbles and rose petals. He turns on some slow jams and helps her undress slowly, he lays her on the bathroom floor and proceeds to taste his wife until her juices flow in his mouth. She screams his name as her eyes roll to the back of her head, he comes back up, kisses her lips and helps her into the tub. He undresses himself and gets in there with her, he hands her a glass of wine and grabs himself a glass. They sat in the tub face to face drinking wine, gazing into one another's eyes. The night had just begun, no distractions.